This book is dedicated to all the Graces in my life:
my daughter Katherine Grace,
my aunt Grace, and my cousin Grace.

—J. M. H.

To my lovely Aunt Honey, for her enduring faith.

—J. G.

Ω

Published by
PEACHTREE PUBLISHERS
1700 Chattahoochee Avenue
Atlanta, Georgia 30318-2112

www.peachtree-online.com

Text © 2006 by Jackie Mims Hopkins
Illustrations © 2006 by Jon Goodell

Book design by Loraine M. Joyner and Jon Goodell

Illustrations created in oils on gessoed cold press illustration board.
Cover marquee typeset in Esselte Letraset Ltd.'s Jazz Plain; interior
title and bylines typeset in Esselte Letraset Ltd.'s Willow; text typeset
in DPT Types Ltd.'s Goudy Infant Regular; incidentals typeset in
Monotype's Century Gothic.

Printed and manufactured in Singapore
10 9 8 7 6 5 4

Library of Congress Cataloging-in-Publication Data

Hopkins, Jackie.
   The gold miner's daughter : a melodramatic fairytale / written
by Jackie Mims Hopkins ; illustrated by Jon Goodell. -- 1st ed.
   p. cm.
   Summary: Gracie Pearl has until sundown to find some gold
to pay the rent to Mr. Bigglebottom, or he will take back the
family gold mine and force her to marry him.
   ISBN 10: 1-56145-362-5
   ISBN 13: 978-1-56145-362-7
   [1. Gold miners--Fiction. 2. Characters in literature--Fiction.]
I. Goodell, Jon, ill. II. Title.
PZ7.H77515Gol 2006
[E]--dc22

2005020581

THE GOLD MINER'S
DAUGHTER
A MELODRAMATIC FAIRY TALE

JACKIE MIMS HOPKINS

ILLUSTRATED BY JON GOODELL

PEACHTREE
ATLANTA

Deep in the heart of gold minin' country lived a hardworking miner and his daughter. Pa and Gracie Pearl had always enjoyed gold minin', but alas, hard times had come upon them.

"Any luck yet, Gracie Pearl?" asked Pa.

"No sir, I'm afraid not. What're we going to do if we can't find any gold in this here mine? We're plumb out of time. That good-for-nothin' banker, Mr. Bigglebottom, will be here any day now to collect his money."

"Don't you worry your pretty little head, daughter. We'll think of something."

"Well, we'd better think of it quicker'n a cockroach when the lights come on," said Gracie Pearl, "because the old buzzard's chuggin' up the hill right now."

"Good afternoon, Gracie Pearl. You're looking lovely as usual," said Mr. Bigglebottom. "Tell me, my sweet, do you have any gold for me?"

"You know I haven't found any yet," said Gracie Pearl. "This mine's as worthless as weevils in cornmeal."

"Mr. Bigglebottom, sir," begged Pa, "if you can give us more time, we'll find a way to pay you."

"How will you be able to pay me *later* if you can't pay me now?" asked the banker.

"Pa's right," said Gracie Pearl. "We'll find a way to pay you if you'll just give us a little more time."

The greedy banker twisted his oily mustache, eyeballed Gracie Pearl, and said to Pa, "I'll give you till sunset. But if you can't pay me, I'll take back the land and your house…and I'll take your daughter for my wife."

"No!" shrieked Gracie Pearl. "I will *never* marry you!"

"We'll just see about that," Mr. Bigglebottom said with an evil laugh. "I'll be back this evening and I'll expect my payment…or my bride."

Once the banker was out of sight,
Gracie Pearl threw one heck of a hissy fit. "His
bride? I'll be his bride—when hound dogs fly!"
she screamed. "I'll never marry that nasty
man and we'll never find anything in this
useless mine, either. I'm going into town
to see if I can find gold
some other way."

Gracie Pearl unhitched Sassafras the pack mule and headed into town.

It wasn't long before Gracie Pearl caught a glimpse of a blonde girl barreling across the road.

"Excuse me," yelled Gracie Pearl. "I'm in a real mess and I need your help. I've got to get ahold of some gold before sunset. Do you know where I can find some?"

"Sorry, lady. I don't have time to stop and chat!" the girl shouted over
her shoulder. "I've got troubles of my own. How was I to know I was eating Mr.
Bigglebottom's porridge? He sicced his bears on me and they're hot on my trail."

"B-B-Bears?" stammered Gracie Pearl. "Bears aren't much better than Mr.
Bigglebottom. Thank you kindly just the same," she called as the girl sped away.

Gracie Pearl urged the mule on. When they reached the outskirts of town, she spotted something just ahead. As they trotted closer, she realized it was three pigs tied to the railroad tracks.

"Help, help!" they squealed.

"What happened?" asked Gracie Pearl, untying the pigs.

"We borrowed money from Mr. Bigglebottom to build our houses. When we couldn't pay him back, he tied us to the tracks," said the first little pig.

"He said he'd make piggy pancakes out of us," cried the second little pig.

"Our mother warned us about the big bad wolf. But he's a puppy dog compared to Bigglebottom," said the third little pig.

Gracie Pearl sighed. "I know what you mean. I've got to get ahold of some gold before sunset. Would you happen to know where I might find some?" she asked as she freed the last little pig.

"Sorry. If we knew where to find gold, we wouldn't have been tied to the tracks," the pig grunted. "Thanks for untying us, though."

"You're welcome," said Gracie Pearl. "Glad I could help."

Gracie Pearl made her way into town and stopped at the Golden Goose Café.

"What'll it be, ma'am?" said the fellow behind the counter.

"I've got to get ahold of some gold before sunset…or I'll be in big trouble," Gracie replied.

"Well," he sighed, "once upon a time, I had me a goose that laid golden eggs."

"Really?" asked Gracie Pearl. "Do you still have her?"

"Unfortunately, I don't. Mr. Bigglebottom took her," he said. "The joke was on him, though, 'cause she stopped laying eggs," he added.

"I don't suppose you still have any of her eggs, do you?" asked Gracie Pearl.

"Sorry. He took those, too. But check around. I seem to remember hearing about someone spinning straw into gold."

"Thank you, sir. I'll keep that in mind."

Gracie Pearl went next door to Spinning Wheels Unlimited and found the beautiful clerk asleep at the counter. Gracie shook her awake and said, "I've got to get ahold of some gold before sunset. Do any of your spinning wheels spin straw into gold?"

"No," said the clerk with a big yawn, "but if you prick your finger on this one, you won't be awake for long."

"Do you know of anyone who can spin straw into gold?" asked Gracie Pearl.

"I do recollect hearing about someone who lived out west of town aways. What was the name?" the clerk said, nodding off again. "I think it began with an *R*…"

"Much obliged," said Gracie Pearl, and she and Sassafras set off toward the setting sun.

When Gracie Pearl got to
Hope Street, she saw a mailbox
in front of a looming tower.
She hurried over and
read the name: *Rapunzel.*

Someone had posted instructions on a
signboard: *To contact resident, yell*
"Rapunzel, Rapunzel, let down your hair!"

So Gracie Pearl hollered at the top of her
lungs. Pretty soon, down, down, down from
a window high above tumbled a long,
golden braid.

"Are you the one who can spin straw into
gold?" shouted Gracie Pearl. "I've got to get
ahold of some gold before sunset!"

"No," said Rapunzel irritably, "but people get the two of us mixed up all the time. In fact, Bigglebottom, that low-down dirty weasel, thought I was the one who could spin straw into gold, so he locked me in this tower with a spinning wheel.

The man you're looking for lives five houses down thataway. His name is Rumplestiltskin."

"Thank you, ma'am," said Gracie. "Sorry to have troubled you."

Gracie Pearl knocked at the fifth house. An odd little lady answered the door.

"Are you Mrs. Rumplestiltskin?" asked Gracie Pearl hopefully. The sun was sinking low in the sky.

"No, I'm his sister, Fiddlesnopskin," replied the woman.

"I've got to get ahold of some gold before sunset," Gracie said frantically. "I heard your brother could spin straw into gold."

Fiddlesnopskin led Gracie out into the yard and showed her a large hole.

"Some time back Rumplestiltskin came home all in a snit," she said. "He was furious because some deal he'd made hadn't worked out. He roared something about Bigglebottom and gold. Then he stomped his feet so hard that the ground cracked open. He fell in the hole and hasn't been seen since."

"Oh no!" cried Gracie Pearl. "Now I'll never get ahold of some gold before sunset. I'm doomed—I'll have to marry creepy old Mr. Bigglebottom."

When Gracie Pearl got home, she found her pa sitting outside the mine in deep despair. Before Gracie Pearl could give Pa the bad news, Mr. Bigglebottom drove up in his sputtering jalopy.

"Well, well," said Mr. Bigglebottom, "do you have that gold to pay me?"

"Not yet," said Pa, "but—"

"But, nothing," interrupted Mr. Bigglebottom. "Now I will take Gracie Pearl for my wife."

"NEVER!" screamed Gracie Pearl.

"Can't you give us just a little more time?" Pa pleaded.

"Time's up, you old goat. Gracie Pearl is mine!" screeched Mr. Bigglebottom.

The dastardly banker grabbed Gracie Pearl's arm and dragged her toward his jalopy.

Pa grabbed Gracie Pearl's other arm and pulled her back. She struggled like a
stuck mule. Her hollerin' could be heard across three counties, and the ground
shook something fierce. She kicked and bucked and stomped her boots as hard as
she could.

Something black and gooey began to gurgle up from under her
boot heel.

As Gracie Pearl broke free from Mr. Bigglebottom's grasp,
a huge gush of the black stuff shot up and blew that rotten
scoundrel clean out of sight.

"Eureka!"
shouted Gracie Pearl
as she and Pa watched
Mr. Bigglebottom
disappear into the clouds.

Yes indeed, Gracie Pearl had found her gold…black gold.
Turns out, there was enough oil on that land
to live happily forever and ever after.